ISIS:

TRIAL OF THE GODDESS

Also by Shawn James

ISIS

The Cassandra Cookbook

All About Marilyn

The Temptation of John Haynes

All About Nikki- The Complete First Season

If you have questions and comments about this book send your E-mails to Shawn James at:

sjsdirectny@aol.com

And check out Shawn James' blog at:

shawnsjames.blogspot.com

ISIS:

TRIAL OF THE GODDESS

Shawn James

That page with the legal stuff on it

Dedicated to my inspiration and my muse.

Acknowledgments

I would like to thank God for helping me write this book. If not for Him, I would have never finished this story. With His help maybe I'll be able to take my craft to the next level.

I'd also like to thank my Mother for supporting me and my writing career all these years.

A special thanks to my brother Steve for inspiring me and giving me hope during some of the hardest times of my life.

I'd also like to thank my sister Shawna for giving me a copy of Syd Field's *Screenplay*. That book helped me learn the basics about screenwriting and helped me learn a whole new set of writing skills.

I'd also like to thank all those wonderful African-American book clubs who took the time to read and review *All About Nikki*. I'm hoping everyone continues to support my writing career with this book.

In addition, I'd like to thank fellow writers Liz Issacs and Francine Craft for their continued support and advice that helped me further develop my writing craft.

Finally, I'd like to thank my POD printer. If not for this great technology, this screenplay would be sitting at the bottom of a closet forgotten for years to come.

Chapter 1

Under the moonlit sky, I look down at the corpses of Klansmen strewn about the grass in my backyard. When my crusade is over these United States will have their benighted and corrupt White leaders replaced with a fair and just order I establish.

I'm sure there'll be retaliation from the Whites to other innocent Negroes in town when they become aware of the retribution I have meted out for myself. As their goddess, I cannot let my brothers and sisters suffer for my actions. Having the power to do something about the inhumane treatment my people suffer I must take final action to end the oppression of the Negro people. Only the total extermination of this White vermin will allow my people to live in peace. They have stolen this land from its rightful owners and brought my people here in bondage. I will remove the White menace from this land and fairly recompense those peoples oppressed under the conditions established by their unjust constitution.

I walk through the dozens of broken carcasses dressed in bloodstained white sheets and hoods over to a small body wrapped tightly in a bloodstained white blanket. I look down at my son and tears well up in my eyes. I would have let them live had they spared you. Now I look forward to making their women see their children like this before I kill them.

Squatting down to examine the body of my son, I see the charred corpse of my late husband Joe hanging on the tree in out backyard out of the corner of my eye. I'll make sure you both have proper burials before I go on my crusade.

I storm over to the smoldering wooden shell that was once our home. Embers of the fire that once destroyed it still glow red in the broken blackened boards lying scattered on the ground and inside the gutted framework. As I step onto the porch, the smoky stench from the wafting smoke is almost unbearable. I must find the shovel to dig their graves.

Entering the doorway, I walk past pieces of a mirror that once sat in our entranceway, broken glass from our window, soot and ash from the fire. I know I left the shovel right next to this mirror. I put it here this morning when Joe gave it to me. I meant to put it back in the shed, but I forgot about it when Joseph started crying. We were doing some chores before going out to the store to buy some things. It still should be here.

The full moon casts down in the house and I see the shovel covered in soot, lying on the floor amidst the broken glass and burned wood planks. As I reach for it, a white light approaches me from out of nowhere. The light grows brighter and larger; I put my hands in front of my face to keep from being blinded by it.

In the instant that the light gets in my eyes my surroundings change. Wherever I am must be a lavish place; I'm standing on gold tiles. I'm familiar with the wall paintings that display the exploits of the gods of ancient Egypt; I've seen them many times in the royal palace of Nubia when I was a little girl. However, this place feels different. Could I have been transported to Heliopolis to join my fellow gods?

I look down the corridor and see a pair of golden doors detailed in raised symbols on the far end. As I start walking towards them, they open and two men approach me.

One of the men is tall, strong, and handsome. He's dressed like a prince in a white pleated kilt, golden pectoral collar and brown sandals. Rings are on his fingers and his golden necklace has an amulet on it in the shape of a falcon. When I look at his face I see myself. We could be twins.

The second man is taller than the first with skin as dark as coal. He must be at least seven feet tall. His muscles are larger and thicker than the other man's; he must be very strong. I can see myself in his somber face as well. He wears brown sandals and a black pleated kilt held up by a pair of purple straps. The only jewelry he wears are the textured gold gauntlets on his wrists and the amulet on his neck that depicts a jackal's head. In his hands are chains. Are these for my enemies?

When I approach the gods they greet me with somber expressions. Are they grieving the loss of my family too?

"Are you Horus?" I ask the handsome man.

"I am." He answers.

"And you are Anubis?" I ask the dark skinned man.

"I am. He answers."

"It is unfortunate that we first meet under these circumstances sister." Horus says. "I regret your reunion with us will not be an amicable one."

Horus grabs my wrists. Anubis clamps the iron chains on them. I struggle to pull away from him as Horus clamps more chains on my ankles.

"Take your hands off me!" I demand. "I haven't done anything wrong!" I demand.

"Goddess Isis, by the authority of the Elders of New Heliopolis I place you under arrest." Horus says.

When he says that I yank at the chains on my arms. However, even with my incredible strength I can't break them. "Under arrest? I haven't done anything wrong!"

Anubis grabs me by the shoulders. His grip is so strong I feel like I'm in a vise. He leans over to address me.

"It would be best if you did not resist us." He whispers in my ear.

The gentle tone of Anubis' deep voice eases my fears. I stop resisting.

"Be silent and comply with us sister. You will be able to explain your case to the elders." Anubis reassures.

I take a deep breath and let it out. I hear my heart racing as Horus and Anubis lead me down the corridor towards the mysterious golden doors to face justice for the crimes I'm accused of.

Chapter 2

I get more and more anxious with each step as we approach the golden doors. I'd think being among my fellow gods for the first time would be the thing making me uneasy. It isn't. What's making me tense is not knowing what offense I violated or how they'll punish me.

When Horus opens the golden doors my body tenses with anticipation about what could possibly be on the other side. It can't be good if it took both of Osiris' sons to escort me here.

I let out a sigh of relief as we step into the room. It's not a jail cell thank God. Behind those large golden doors is a large room decorated with the same wall paintings as the corridor. On each side of the golden doors we passed through are several rows of wooden pews. In the center of the room is a large golden bench like the one judges sit at. Anubis did say that the elders would hear my case; it looks like they're allowing me to have a day in court.

I take deep breaths as Horus and Anubis lead me down the aisle into the center of the room in front of the golden bench. Horus then leaves my side and walks through the pair of golden doors behind the bench. A few minutes pass before he returns. As he stands at my side I'm awe-struck. Dozens of deities I only heard about in childhood stories walk past me and take their places in the trial that's about to start.

Five older looking gods take seats behind the bench. Two are old women; three are old men. The oldest looking man sits in the center of the bench. He's bald except for a white beard that frames his dark face. He's dressed in a red caftan and purple robe that make his tall strong frame look all the more intimidating. On his right side sits one of the old women. She wears a sky blue gown and her hair is as white as a cloud. Next to her sits a man with gray skin with a texture like a stone. He's clean-shaven and the chiseled lines in his hard face make him look more rugged. The charcoal caftan and black robe he wears remind me of the ground. On the left side of the old man with the beard sits another woman who is a bit younger than the other three. She wears a white gown and black pectoral collar. The middle-aged man sitting next to her has gray hair cut short to the scalp. He wears a white kilt, gold pectoral collar and a white shawl. When he smiles at me I look away.

I watch as the other gods take their place in the courtroom. One young woman wearing a short blue dress with a large white ostrich feather in her hair takes a seat at the small table next to the judge's bench with the scroll. A stout dark skinned man dressed in a white caftan and scarlet robe stands next to a pair of thrones across from the judge's bench.

The room falls silent as two deities enter the room and approach the thrones. A tall voluptuous bronze skinned woman dressed in pleated white gown, jeweled golden pectoral collar, bracelets and sandals eases into her seat. The confident way she carries herself tells me that she's Queen of New Heliopolis. She smiles at me as the Pharaoh flops into the throne next to hers. He isn't dressed as formally as she is for court. The dowdy white caftan and green robe he has on are what a common man would wear. The only gold he wears is on his belt. When I look at his somber face I'm shocked. Could this man be my father?

The remaining gods take their seats in the gallery behind me. When the stout man standing next to the bench speaks the whole room becomes silent. The young woman at the small table pulls the feather from her hair and starts writing on the scroll.

"Court is now in session." He says. "All are to remain in the courtroom until directed to leave by the Elders."

"Thank you Thoth." The old man sitting at the center of the bench says. "Present the charges brought against the goddess."

"Great Ra, Isis the daughter of the Pharaoh Osiris and the Nubian Keer-Sheba is charged with allowing hatred into her heart. She is also charged with forsaking her Heliopolitan heritage and worshipping another God."

Ra looks down at me. His intense glare pierces me to the soul. I put on my bravest face and make eye contact with him as he addresses me.

"These are serious charges goddess. How do you answer them?" Ra asks.

That's a good question. I don't know much about the law except what my late husband Joe taught me. And I doubt American legal arguments would be effective in a Heliopolitan court. Sure I can defend myself against murder charges, but how do I defend myself against being accused of having hatred in my heart and my religious beliefs? What would I plead to such abstract charges? Would guilty or not guilty even be a valid plea in such a case?

I decide to risk it and say not guilty. Before I can speak the Queen jumps off her throne and rushes over to stand beside me.

"Great Ra, Isis has no understanding of our system of laws. She was born of a mortal woman and raised in mortal culture." She says.

Ra cuts a harsh look at the queen. I don't think they like each other.

"It is no concern of yours Isis." Ra says. "A New Heliopolitan whether birthed by goddess or mortal is under the jurisdiction of judgment by the Elders. She will state her case."

I'm about to speak for myself for the second time when Queen Isis gives me a stern look that makes me decide to remain silent.

"Elders, I only ask for a few days to teach Isis about our laws." Isis says. "From my instruction she will be able to defend herself in our court."

"Isis why involve yourself in this proceeding?" The stone-faced man says. "Out of all of us it should be you who would most want to see this goddess face punishment."

Isis scowls at the old man before she speaks. "Elders, it would be unjust for us to try Isis without giving her an opportunity to understand the charges and the concepts behind the laws she is accused of violating. I only ask for some time to prepare her so that she can have a fair trial in our court."

The Elder gods confer among themselves before Ra speaks.

"We will grant you the remainder of this day to prepare your case Isis." Ra says. "Because the goddess is not educated in our laws, she will not speak for herself in these proceedings. You will be her counsel in this case. Whatever judgment the she receives will be based upon your defense."

Isis looks directly into Ra's eyes. The smile she gives him lets him know that she's not afraid of him. That scares the crap out of me.

"Thank you great Ra." Isis says politely.

"If that is all then court will be adjourned." Ra says. "We will reconvene here tomorrow at this time."

The gods get up out of the pews and walk through the doors I came through. The Elders leave the bench and walk through the doors behind their bench. Thoth and the woman with the feather follow them. In a few minutes the room is empty of all the gods except for members of the royal family and myself.

I wonder what they're going to do with me. What do gods do with their prisoners? Are Horus and Anubis going to take me to a deep dark cell somewhere until court starts again?

"Mother, where shall I escort Isis?" Anubis asks.

"Take her to my quarters." Isis says.

Horus gives his mother a perplexed look. He's probably wondering why she's helping me. I'd like the answer to that question myself.

"Mother, what are you doing?" He asks. "Why are you involving yourself in this trial? Gods have to defend themselves in court."

"She cannot defend herself in these proceedings son. And since her father will not protect her I shall." Isis says glaring at the man sitting in the throne.

The Queen takes my hand and leads me around the bench and through the golden doors. Horus and Anubis follow us. As we go through the doors, I look back and see my father still sitting in his throne quietly with a forlorn look on his face. I wish he had said something too.

Chapter 3

Half a day isn't much time to prepare Isis for trial in the court of the Elder gods. I have a lot to do and I'll have to work quickly. My knowledge of Heliopolitan law isn't as extensive as Osiris or Thoth but Isis will be better off than facing the Elders alone. We can put an adequate defense together if she cooperates with me. Maybe we can even save her life.

I know Ra and the Elder gods hide their murderous intentions behind legal procedures. This trial is a legal formality so they can have the justification to do what they wish. They planned on executing Isis the moment they brought her back here. There's no way Isis could have defended herself fairly; had the naive girl spoken just now she would have signed her own death warrant.

The Elder gods always felt that Isis would be a danger to all around her. They thought her human upbringing would corrupt her and eventually lead to her betraying us. The only reason they let her live is because Osiris loved her so much. However, Isis didn't start out being a threat to mankind. She only became a danger to others because of our centuries of indifference. It was our fault that she killed those men. Had we not abandoned her she would have not gone astray.

The Elders were wrong to think I would go along with this farce of a trial and condone the execution of Isis because she's the child of Osiris' adulterous affair. I hold no ill feelings against Isis; I love her as much as my own son. I had hoped Osiris would care enough to have the courage to speak on our daughter's behalf. Unfortunately, like everyone else at the trial he let the farce continue. I'm disappointed in him most of all. He could have stopped this before it all started.

Following me to my quarters, Horus and Anubis flank Isis' sides. As we enter the royal bedchamber, I focus on the tasks at hand. We can plan a legal strategy later. Right now I have to get her out of those bloody clothes and into something fresh.

"Anubis unlock Isis' chains." I request.

"Mother, I don't think that would be wise." Horus protests.

"Son, as long as your sister is in my presence she is a guest." I say. "I will provide her with the same generous hospitality you and your family would receive during a visit to the palace."

"But mother, she's a murderer." Horus says. "She could-"

"Isis will not harm me Horus." I reply.

"How can you be so sure? She tore people apart." Horus continues.

"Horus, this is not the court of the Elders." I demand. "Now I have much work to do and I can't do it until Anubis unlocks those chains."

Horus grimaces at me. I appreciate his concern, but he has no need to worry about my safety. Isis has no intention of harming me. She's thinking more about those she's lost and the upcoming trial, not planning the murder of us all. My son should not be so eager to take everything the Elders tell him to heart. Sometimes their stories are just stories.

Anubis eagerly unlocks the chains. He sees what I see, that Isis is no threat to me. "You'll be fine sister." He says. "Will that be all Mother?"

"That will be all." I reply.

My sons take their leave. I clap my hands and two servants walk into the room. The women close the door behind them and await my instructions.

"Take Isis into the cistern and draw a bath." I say to one of the women. "I will be there shortly."

"Lay out my new kilt and short blouse." I tell the other. "And lay out my white gown. Have them ready for us when we finish bathing."

"Mistress, two garments?" One of the servants asks.

"Yes. One set of garments is for me and the other is for my daughter." I say. "Have that- gown she's wearing destroyed."

As the servants take Isis out of the room, Osiris rushes in full of the anger he should have directed at the Elders. I don't have time to argue with him. I've got to prepare to join Isis at the cistern.

"What do you think you're doing interfering in the court of the elders?" He barks at me.

"What you wouldn't do." I order taking off my crown. "Standing up for our daughter."

"Isis is a grown woman. She can stand trial for herself." Osiris says.

"That trial is a farce and you know it." I reply.

"It's out of my hands. I can't judge my own daughter. That's the law of the Elder gods-"

"But you could have spoken for her." I reply taking off my earrings. "The Elders plan to kill your own child and you sit there and allow it to happen-"

"I'm following the law. I can't interfere in their court. Especially in the trial of one of my own family members-"

"You're as bad as they are hiding behind legal procedures like a coward." I snap yanking bracelets and armlets off my arms and wrists. "Sanctioning the murder of our own child-"

"What business of it is yours?" Osiris orders. "She lived her life the wrong way and now she's paying for it."

"We put her on that path."

"With Isis' life on the line this isn't time for one of your maverick stunts." Osiris demands. "You know Ra doesn't like you. If your defense fails, Isis could die."

"It doesn't change anything."

"Her death will be on your head."

"Like I said Osiris, it doesn't change anything."

Osiris stands behind me to help me remove my pectoral collar. He may disagree with me but he is going to support me in helping our daughter.

"You are one stubborn woman. That's why I love you so much." He says kissing my neck. "Isis is lucky to have you at her side."

"I hope I can adequately defend her."

"I'm more worried about the Elders." Osiris laughs. "Whenever you're determined like this nothing can stop you. Not even them and they know it."

"I got lucky back then." I say. "I'll need that luck again if I'm going to win this case."

"If it wasn't for your faith I wouldn't be standing here." Osiris says. "I know you'll win."

Chapter 4

I thought that the mentioning of a second goddess Isis in one of the ancient texts was an error by the scribes. That obscure reference must have some merit because the goddess is standing right in front of me.

From the vague passage I read this morning in the Library of the Legion, this Isis was supposed to be the daughter born to Osiris sired through a Nubian slave some years after the end of the Heliopolitan War on the ninth day of the ninth month of the year A.D. 73. The scribe speculated that the woman had lived her whole life as a slave and died unaware of her godly lineage. It seems his assumptions were wrong. Almost two eons later the goddess still lives.

I didn't think much of that obscure reference until I came upon the lynching of a Negro family. I soon became suspicious of the woman watching her react to the death of her child. It surprised me that she didn't succumb to the overwhelming number of men attacking her and it was more bizarre to see this one woman overpower the whole mob. I've never seen a mortal display such incredible feats of strength and speed; she did things only gods have power to do. The fierce way she brutally slaughtered her foes with her bare hands showed the expertise of a warrior who mastered her fighting techniques. Seeing her in action made me think about that ancient text I read this morning. I had to learn more about her.

I was about to approach the woman she was enveloped in the flash of light that the gods use to travel with. This development only made the mysteries regarding her all the more intriguing. Determined to get answers to my many questions, I followed her through the portal to New Heliopolis. My suspicions were confirmed when Thoth read the charges against her. This woman is the lost daughter of Osiris!

Not to arouse the suspicions of the other gods, I quickly used my magic to disguise myself as a servant so I could observe the trial. It was a good strategic move; the Queen's handmaid assigned me to the detail of her bathing attendants. Escorting Isis to the cistern, I got a good look at her. She looks just like her father.

Isis is still in a severe state of shock. She stares down at the white marble floor like she's in a trance. I wouldn't be in my right mind either if someone killed my child in front of me. It was disturbing to watch them kill her baby; it made me cringe and I've seen almost every form of depravity known to man. I want to express my condolences to Isis but I can't say anything. I have to keep my cover so I can continue observing the trial.

The other servant pulls a lever on the wall and the large circular pool in the center of the room begins to fill with steaming water. Before she leaves, she points to Isis and gestures at me. I guess I have the grim task of undressing the goddess.

Perhaps it's best that I'm here to do this job; I'm quite used to the smell of fresh blood and the sight of it. With the blood still wet, I can easily tear this gown off her. I reach for the top of the gown and yank at it. The bloody cotton material tears down the center like I wanted it to. I get behind her, peel off the blood soaked garment, and rush out into the corridor.

There isn't anyone around to see me so I'll quickly dispose of this rag using my own power. A burst of blue flame erupts from my palms and vaporizes the garment in seconds. I'm impressed. My control over the hellfire is so precise that I can't even smell a trace of smoke in the air.

I quickly return to the cistern. The pool hasn't filled completely with water yet, and the other servant hasn't returned. Lucky for Isis the blood hasn't begun drying, it should be easy to clean off her once we get her in the water. I feel like I really want to say something, but I can't blow my cover.

The air in the room is tense until other servant returns with a large wooden box. She opens it up to reveal a group of bottles and washcloths. She pulls a green alabaster bottle out of the box and pours its oil into the water. Soon the room begins to smell like flowers. She gestures to me. I look down into the cistern and notice that it's almost ready. I guess she wants me to help Isis into the water.

I decide to test the water myself before letting the goddess go in. Reaching into the steaming pool with my foot, I let my toes test the temperature of the water. It's not too hot. Just as I'm about to lead Isis into the water the Queen enters the cistern dressed in her white linen bathrobe. If she's going to bathe her, then there's something behind it. The Queen is a cunning woman and she's definitely using the intimacy of the bath to secretly discuss legal strategy with Isis. I'm anxious to hear what they have to say to each other.

Queen Isis takes off her robe, hands it to the servant and gestures for us to leave. As we rush out of the cistern, the Queen closes the door behind us. I hide my disappointment behind a servant's stoic facial expression.

Chapter 5

With the servants gone, I take Isis' hand and lead her down the steps into the steaming water. I should have her cleaned up in no time.

When we're in the bath, I reach over to the wooden box at the edge of the pool and pull out a washcloth and a bottle of cleansing cream. As I wash Isis' face she turns away from me keeping her eyes on the water. I know she's still grieving over her losses, but this is no time for her to be withdrawn. In this time of crisis she must have courage.

When I finish washing Isis' face I catch her eyes. She turns away again, but then starts to look at me when she catches my kind smile. "I'm sorry about what happened to your family." I tell her.

"I'm sorry too." Isis mutters shyly.

"I know you're going through a lot. But have to keep your head held up through it all. A goddess always stands with her head held high."

"I have a lot on my mind." Isis sighs.

"The situation you're in is troubling." I reply. "But in this time of crisis you have to be strong. This is no time to fall apart."

"I want to curl up in a ball and hide. This whole trial is scary to think about."

"I understand your fears Isis." I say. "And it's okay to be afraid. But you must work past your fear."

"Are you scared?" Isis asks.

"I'm terrified." I answer smiling.

"How do you stay so confident in the middle of so much trouble?"

"I won't be able to accomplish anything if I let my fear overtake me. And accomplishing my goals are far more important than what I'm afraid of."

"What do you want from me?"

"I want to prepare you to face this trial. However, I can only do that with your help."

"I definitely want your help. I don't know anything about this place." Isis says. "But could you explain why I've got to hold my head up?"

"By holding your head high you can see a solution. When one looks down all they see is a problem overwhelming them."

Isis picks up her head. "Since I'm a goddess I have to face this like a goddess. This trial is going to go on whether I'm prepared or not. I'd rather be prepared for it."

Even though Isis speaks confidently, I can still see the fear in her eyes. She's forcing herself to work past all her fear and grief. I'm proud of her for being so courageous.

As I'm scrubbing her back, Isis turns and takes the washcloth from me. She even tries to force a smile out of herself. "I can finish up myself."

"Are you sure?"

"You've done a lot for me already. The least I can do is finish washing up."

"Do you want to be alone?"

"No."

"I guess I'm in a lot of trouble." Isis sighs.

"That's an understatement." I reply. "As Ra stated, these are serious charges."

"Why? Hatred in my heart and worshipping God isn't harmful to anyone." Isis pleads. "I could see a harsh penalty for killing those men, but not how I feel and think."

"Unfortunately, the standard in the realm of the gods is much higher than in the realm of mortals. Simple sins to mortals can be a heinous crime to gods."

"These laws are all so abstract." Isis blurts.

"The power of a goddess is abstract." I reply. "Beings such as us have powers far greater than man. The way we think can affect the way we act. And those actions can have a tremendous impact on all of those around us."

"I take it if we think wrong-"

"The ramifications of the decisions made on those thoughts or feelings could impact civilizations of peoples for eons."

"I never thought about it that way. All I can think about is the hurt inside me."

"That's because of your mortal upbringing. In time you'll come to understand like we do."

"You talk like we've got a chance of winning this trial."

"I have faith."

"Well, I like to be realistic." Isis says. "What's the worst that can happen to me if I'm found guilty?"

"The offenses you are being charged with are punishable by death."

Isis gasps and grabs her chest. She then takes a deep breath and lets it out. I see her gesturing to put her head down but she keeps her eyes on me.

"I'm not going to let them kill you." I say.

Isis gives me a skeptical look. I don't think she believes me. I'll have to believe for both of us.

Once all the blood is washed off Isis' body, she takes a deep breath before she leans forward to dunk her head in the murky chest deep water. I know she wants to do things for herself, but it would be best if I washed her hair. The blood is in some hard to reach places of her scalp. Since I'm taller than her, I think I can reach it better than she can.

"Hold on- let me wash your hair." I request.

"That's okay. I can wash my own hair."

"There's blood in some difficult to reach places."

Isis trusts me, she leans back and I take her head in my hands. When her hair is wet I reach behind me for the bottle of cleansing cream and smear a small drop of it on the top of her scalp. When it foams into lather I start massaging it into her chestnut curls. Isis closes her eyes so that the soap doesn't get in them.

"Those Elders are really intimidating." Isis continues. "One of them was staring right through me."

"Ra's presence can strike fear in even a god." I reply. "However, you never defer to him or any other god. When you address him look him directly in the eye."

"But he's an Elder. I was always taught to defer to my Elders."

"In our realm he has to show you the same respect you show him."

"I guess I have to keep my head up."

"Always." I say. "Are you ready to come out?"

"Yes." Isis answers. "Just let me rinse my hair."

"You can do that in the shower."

"What's a shower?" Isis asks.

"A quick way to get cleaned up. Anubis built it when he renovated or baths sometime ago."

Isis and I step out of the murky pool of water and stand under the golden falcon's heads on the left wall of the cistern. When I pull the lever Isis is surprised when warm water sprays out of the sculptures mouth all over her body. The soap washes out of her hair and runs into the drain beneath her feet. I approach the door and let the servants know we've finished bathing.

The servants enter the room and wrap me in my robe. They wrap a linen cloth around Isis and another around her hair. We leave the cistern and head for my quarters.

TRIAL OF THE GODDESS

Now that I've had a chance to get to know her a little better we can plan our strategy for court.

Chapter 6

I'm feeling a little better now. The bath helped me relieve some of the stress I've been feeling about this trial. I'm still a little scared, but I feel I can work through it.

Queen Isis and I walk a short distance down the hall from the cistern to her quarters. As we enter her room, I take in the luxurious furnishings. I was pretty out of it before; the only things I saw before were the mosaic tiles on the floor and the leopard skin rugs. This room has furnishings fit for royalty. I wonder where I'll be sleeping.

I notice two sets of clothes lying on the bed. One set of clothes is a white pleated gown and the other is a short while linen wrap kilt and sleeveless shirt. Isis picks up the pleated gown; so I'll assume the kilt and blouse are for me.

I pull the wraps from around my body and hair and quickly get dressed.

These New Heliopolitan clothes fit strangely; the hem of my blouse hits right above my navel. And the kilt is so loose in the waist; if it weren't for my hips holding it up it'd fall right off me. And the hem of my skirt- It falls at the midpoint of my thighs! I'm more appalled at the sight of myself in the mirror. Are these clothes or underwear?

Okay, I'm sounding pretty ungrateful for someone who was wearing a blood soaked nightgown a few minutes ago. I should be thankful the Queen is giving me one of her outfits to wear. Anything in her closet would be better than standing trial in front of the Elders in my birthday suit. And I shouldn't be so shocked that the hemline of my skirt is so short; I wore clothing like this in Nubia when I was younger. Much younger. Like when I was fourteen.

Then again, New Heliopolis isn't like America where women wear skirts to their ankles; in my short time here I've seen hemlines on the goddesses' dresses here vary from midthigh to ankle lengths. Taking another look at this outfit it's kind of cute. It makes me look at least a thousand or so years younger.

Queen Isis pulls her gown over her head and smiles at me. She's proud of the way I look. I'm still getting used to it.

"You look beautiful." The Queen says.

"I feel like I'm in my underwear." I blurt.

"Are you uncomfortable? I do have other garments."

"No, no this is fine." I say smiling at The Queen. "I like it. It's just- where I used to live, we wore skirts down to our ankles."

"Most girls your age wear garments like this." Queen Isis replies. "What makes you so uncomfortable in it?"

"I'm comfortable in it." I say. "I just haven't worn anything like this in centuries. It's going to take some getting used to again."

I'm curious about something. The Queen is definitely older than me and she says these clothes are for a New Heliopolitan girl my age. If that's the case, why does she have this outfit in her wardrobe?

"You're older than me. And this outfit is for a girl my age. Where would you wear this?" I ask.

"Osiris liked it." she answers smiling at me.

"That man who was sitting on the throne with you. Is he Osiris?"

"Yes, that's your father."

"He's probably ashamed of me."

"Your father loves you very much. He just has a hard time expressing his feelings."

I don't believe that, his actions speak louder than her words. I'm the child of an adulterous relationship between a god and a mortal. When he sees me he sees a mistake he made a long time ago. That's why he hasn't extended a hand to help me.

"I think he'd be happy if I died."

"Don't say that."

"His life would be a lot easier with the child of his mistress gone."

"I don't want to hear you talk like this. Your father would be very sad if you died."

I decide not to say anymore. It just hurts too much to think about my father and how I came into this world. I hate learning that my mother is a whore and my father could give less than a damn about me. The whole situation is frustrating to think about. In all the days of my life I've never even known who my father is. And now when I need him most he avoids me. What makes things so frustrating is that I want to be angry about this whole situation but I can't. I need to keep my head up and focused on facing the Elders.

Queen Isis notices the grimace on my face. She smiles at me and gives me a hug. "How you came into this world isn't important. We all love you very much."

"I don't think I could forgive a man if he betrayed me like that." I reply.

"I no longer think about my husband's affairs." Queen Isis says breaking the embrace. "So don't concern yourself with them. Focus on getting through this trial."

"What's our defense?"

"All we can do is tell the truth."

"That isn't much of a defense. I hated those people I killed and I do worship God."

"The truth is that you were raised by mortals in their ways." Isis replies. "You only violated the law because you did not know about it."

"So I am guilty."

"Of violating the law yes. However, we are guilty of not teaching you in the right way. For that your punishment should not be so severe."

"I'm still guilty. I'm still going to die."

"I believe I can convince the Elders to spare your life. You didn't act maliciously, and you've led a good life up until this moment. For those reasons you should be given a chance to redeem yourself."

"What would happen if the elders believed your arguments?"

"I can't say. They may still execute you or they may imprison you."

I thought I was fighting for something. Even if Isis wins her case I still lose. In between two unfavorable judgments, Death is the best of my options. It's quick and final and I know where I'm going. Prison on the other hand is a horrifying endless torture. Most of the people I used to know who came out of prison were never the same once they returned to society. I don't know if I could survive the experience of a Heliopolitan prison and maintain my sanity.

"Why even prepare a defense if I have no chance of winning?" I snap.

"Isis, it's never over until you give up."

"With those two choices as my options I was better off letting the Klansmen lynch me."

"You didn't think you were going to come out of this without some type of punishment-"

"I thought you were defending my life. No matter what happens I'm not gong to be free."

"You'll have a chance to be free once you're redeemed."

"That's not much of a chance. Prison changes people."

"I believe in that chance. You believe in it too."

I'm about to say something when Osiris enters the room. He looks at Isis then looks at me briefly before looking away. He must despise the sight of me.

"Isis- I see you're busy." He says. "I'll come back later."

Osiris dashes out of the room quickly. Isis sighs and then frowns. I'm glad to know that I'm not the only one disappointed with the way my father treats me.

"You better get some rest. The trial will start in a few hours."

I won't argue with her. I don't even know what time it is here. All I know is when I was last in the world I got up with the sun yesterday morning. And when the Klan attacked our home it was half past eight. So I've been up for a long time.

"Where will I sleep?" I ask.

"You can sleep here." Isis replies pointing to the bed.

"Your bed? Where are you going to sleep?"

"This palace has many rooms. Osiris and I will find one to suit us."

As I slide into the center of the bed, Isis gathers her jewels, bracelets, armlets, pectoral collar and crown and places them on a tray sitting on one of the wooden boxes. Before she leaves Isis gives me a kiss on the forehead. When she closes the door, all the candles in the room extinguish themselves and the room goes dark. I close my eyes and try to get whatever moments of sleep that I can. I have a big day ahead of me.

Chapter 7

I lay on the bed staring at the ceiling. Anxiety about tomorrow has me so nervous I can't sleep at all. This is my last day as a free woman and it may be very well my last day alive.

I have to thank God for speaking to Queen Isis' heart to help me get through this. That Heliopolitan woman has been more Christian to me than anyone I've ever known. It takes a tremendous amount of courage to support the daughter of your husband's mistress. I have never seen someone share themselves so selflessly when it would have been easier for them to turn the other cheek and walk away. From cleaning me up, to giving me the clothes on my back, and discussing legal strategy, Queen Isis has done a tremendous job to prepare me for a trial we're going to lose. It takes even more courage to defend a woman who is clearly guilty. She believes that prison will eventually set me free, I have to trust her. I don't have any other options.

Everything Isis has done for me just makes me so much angrier with my father. If Osiris owned up to his responsibilities like a man over a thousand years ago I wouldn't be in this mess. It should have been him getting out of that throne to defend me instead of his wife. The coward sits in his throne with his head down ashamed of me. He has some nerve to be ashamed of me; I'm more ashamed of him than he is of me. I didn't have the affair with my mother, he did. Some Pharaoh he is. An adulterer and a coward who has failed his kingdom and his family. His Queen is a far better leader than he ever will be.

What makes me angry most of all is that I have so many questions to ask Osiris. Because he won't talk to me, I'll never know why my mother had an affair with him. What could he possibly have promised her that she would give herself to him? Why would he need to have an affair with her when he had such a great wife at home? Did he ever love my mother the same way he loved her? Could he have ever loved me at any time in my life? What was I supposed to be the goddess of anyway? This is my life; I deserve to know the truth about it. God, I wish my father would tell me everything he knows.

I wonder if Joe and Joseph made it into Heaven. I wish I had gotten the chance to bury them. They're good people; they don't deserve to be food for the vultures. I can only hope the Negro townspeople will do what I can't.

I hope the Negroes in town don't have to suffer for what I've done. Without me there to protect them, the

Whites in town are sure to massacre them for the justice I served on their leaders. Dozens of Negro people will die without my help. I hate abandoning them the way Osiris abandoned me. There's still much work for me to do for them.

So many questions and no answers to any of them. So much to do and not enough time to do it. That's the story of my life...

Chapter 8

The last time I saw Isis she was just a baby in her mother's arms. I was looking forward to seeing what type of woman my daughter had grown up to become. I was mortified when I saw her standing before the elders bloody and in chains. I couldn't stand to look at her. The sight of my daughter as a prisoner makes me want to cry.

It upsets me to see Isis return to us in such an ignominious fashion. I wish I could have been planning a huge party to celebrate her return instead of helplessly watching her stand trial. I would have gotten up to defend her, but the laws of the Elders tied my hands. As Pharaoh, I can't interfere in their court during the trial of a member of my own family. It tears me up inside knowing that legal procedure keeps me from being close to my daughter when she needs me most. I hated abandoning Isis again; unfortunately, it's the only way she'll receive a fair trial.

Since my argument with my wife, I've been doing what little I can to help. I thought that by going to the library to review the trial of Seth I'd find some fact that Isis could use to help my daughter. Unfortunately, the precedent established in the trial of Seth assures the only way this trial can conclude is with Isis' conviction. Looking at the evidence in Seth's case and the facts in Isis' case, it would take a miracle for my wife to convince the elders to change their original interpretation of the law.

I was going to talk to Isis about my research, however when I returned to our quarters she was discussing legal strategy with our daughter. I didn't want to interfere in their counseling session, so I quickly left and returned to the library when I saw them talking. My wife has been hard on me since this trial began. She thinks that I'm indifferent to Isis when I'm doing everything in my power to make sure I won't have to plan our daughter's funeral.

I look up at the weapons displayed on the North wall of the study. Framed in a mahogany display case are a golden bow, a quiver of solid gold arrows, a golden spear, a pair of golden gauntlet bracelets, a gold shield, and an electrum sword. Most of the gods believe these weapons are display pieces meant to brighten up the room. Only my wife and I know I was to give Isis these weapons when she came of age. When I couldn't find her I put them here as a tribute to her memory. When she was a baby I looked forward to the day when she could hold them in her hands. Now that she is back among us I still look forward to the day when she can wield them.

I hear footsteps approaching. I turn around and see Isis approaching me. The aggravated look on her face tells me she's looking for a fight. I don't want to argue; our approaches may be different but our goals are the same. I'd best explain my way of doing things so we can come to an understanding.

"I thought I'd find you here." Isis says.

"How is Isis?" I ask.

"Sleeping." Isis answers. "Why did you leave so abruptly?"

"I didn't want to interfere with your counseling session."

"You know Isis thinks you're ashamed of her."

"Her perceptions of me are wrong." I say. "As are yours."

"Your actions speak louder than your words Osiris. You haven't lifted a finger to help her since the elders arrested her."

"If you look at my actions, you'll see I'm doing the right thing." I continue. "I want my daughter to have a fair trial. For that to happen I must follow the law."

"Do you always have to hide behind the law?"

"With my daughter's life on the line I don't want any mistakes."

"There won't be any. I'm not as well versed as you in the law but I believe my defense will save Isis' life."

"What's your plan?" I ask.

"I'm going to try to convince the Elders that Isis isn't a danger to us the way Seth was."

"It's a good argument. She isn't the menace my brother was."

"Isis is sure she's going to die."

"I believe she has a chance of surviving." Osiris continues. "If the Elders can spare the life of an evil man like Seth, than they should let my daughter live. Her crimes are far less egregious than anything he's done."

"I agree. Our brother deserved his fate. But Isis doesn't deserve Seth's punishment."

"Unfortunately the Elders judge both man and god harshly by the same set of unyielding rules."

"True, their interpretations of the law are extreme, but perhaps we can get them to compromise for once."

"So what were you doing here?"

"Looking for a precedent that would get you the compromise you seek." I answer. "Reading the transcripts of Seth's trial, I couldn't find anything there to help Isis."

"I thought you were here wallowing in self pity."

"I don't want to see Isis die either." I say. "You know, we're both on the same side."

"I know." Isis replies. "But sometimes you're so wrapped up in procedure-"

"That it seems I don't have any feeling." I continue. "She is my daughter and I do love her. This is as much my fight as it is yours."

Isis and I look up at the weapons in the display case. I let out a sigh.

"I always wanted to share them with Isis." I say.

"One day you shall."

"I believe I will. They're the only things that have given me hope through the years." I continue. "Whenever I'd wonder what she was doing in the world I would come to this case and think about her."

"You'd probably like that." Isis says taking my hand.

"I'd like for this trial to be over." I say clasping it tight.

"Me too."

Silently, I say a prayer to the God that my daughter worships. I don't care if it's a crime in the eyes of the Elders. It's beyond my power to help her; I can only trust in him to save her life.

Chapter 9

The charred remains of my husband's body swing from the rope hung over the oak tree in our yard. Three Klansmen grab me and force me to watch the carnage while the mob celebrates. I clutch my baby tightly in my arms as they cackle in delight over his death.

"Ain't seen an educated nigger yet smart enough to figger his way out of a noose" One of the men taunts.

In the midst of their depraved celebration, the men laugh as they turn to me. They taunt me making kissing sounds. One man puts his hands under my chin and forces me to stare into his cold green eyes. I clutch my baby tightly to my chest.

"I bet you taste sweet." He says.

"Been wanting a piece of that since it came to town." Another hollers.

I have to get away; from them before they act on the twisted ideas inside their imaginations. Somehow I manage to break out of their grip. I bolt for the woods, but I'm grabbed from behind. There are too many of them, I can't get away. I clutch my baby tightly to my chest.

Tears run down my cheeks as I hear hollers and laughter. Joseph cries as the ringleader of the mob approaches us. The big fat man's breath stinks of whiskey. He raises the butt of his shotgun and slams it into the bundle in my hands. Joseph doesn't get a chance to scream.

I'm grabbed by the shoulders and shoved into the mob. "YA'LL WANNA FUCK THIS BITCH 'FORE WE KILL HER!" The ringleader demands.

The men charge towards me making taunts and kissing sounds. I feel them pinching my breasts and buttocks as I look down at my baby's broken body in a bloodstained blanket. Everything turns black as my screams wake me from the nightmare.

I still feel drowsy, but I'm too scared to go back to sleep. I don't want to risk having that nightmare again. I don't want to go there. But I don't want to be here either.

I stare at the ceiling thinking about the only outcome of this trial, my conviction. I've come to terms with the fact that I am going to pay for what I've done. I've done wrong and it's only right that I be punished for it. Whatever the penalty is I'm ready to face it like a goddess and a woman.

If I had to pick my own punishment, I'd prefer imprisonment over death. I really don't want to die; that was my fear getting the better of me. I was scared of facing the unknown. I don't know what their interpretation of prison is or what to expect; I don't even know what's going to happen in the next minute here. All I know is that without something to hope for I may as well give up and I'm not doing that. I have to believe in the chance offered to me by Queen Isis. Imprisonment may be the scariest of my options but it's the only one that allows me to look forward to being a free woman again.

I wonder what time it is. If there were a window in the room I could tell by the way the sun or the moon was set in the sky. Unfortunately, this room has none so I can't tell if it's day or night. I can't even hear what's going on outside in the hallway. In some ways it's like a tomb.

My train of thought is broken when the door opens and all the candles in the room light up. I spring up to greet Isis. She's got all her jewelry and make-up on. It must be time for us to go to court. I'm ready.

"Good morning Isis. How did you sleep?"

"Fine." I lie.

"Are you ready for court?"

"Yes."

Isis lets me out of the room and closes the door behind us. I follow her down the long empty corridor and then through the two large golden doors into the courtroom. All of the gods observing the trial are already here, and the goddess with the feather in her hair is sitting at her desk. Thoth stands next to the bench of the elders and Horus and Anubis stand in front of the other set of golden doors behind us. Standing beside them are the two servants who helped me in the cistern. As we walk over to the space in front of the Elders bench I notice Osiris sitting in his throne. He's still somber, however he seems focused. When I look at him he doesn't put his head down. Instead he gives me an indifferent look.

When Isis and I are standing directly in front of the Elders bench, Thoth walks through the doors behind the bench. Soon he returns and the elder gods take their seats behind the bench. I put my hands in front of me and look the Elders directly in their eyes as Thoth calls the court to order.

"Court is now in session." He says. "All are to remain in the courtroom until directed to leave by the Elders."

Ra gives us both a cold glare before he speaks. "Thoth could you state the case against the goddess once more."

"The goddess Isis, daughter of the Pharaoh Osiris and concubine Keer-Sheba is charged with allowing hatred in her heart. She is also charged with forsaking her heritage and worshipping another God."

"Present your evidence on the first count Thoth." Ra requests.

Hold on. I thought we were supposed to go first. Yesterday Ra seemed eager for me to speak first. Why the sudden change of procedure? Perhaps the Elders were taking advantage of my ignorance in the hopes of ending this trial with an early conviction. Thank God Isis stepped in and put a stop to their scheme. Maybe now I can get a fair trial.

When I hear that Thoth is presenting his case before ours I unconsciously react by grimacing. Isis gives me a friendly look and I relax. I'm glad they're doing it this way; it makes more sense to me. At least I'll know what the basis of their case is about before Isis replies to the charges.

Thoth walks to the center of the floor in front of the bench and presents his facts. The woman at the small desk takes the feather out of her hair and begins writing.

"Elders, a chronicle of Isis' recent actions will show that she has maliciously slaughtered dozens of White men in America." Thoth begins. "Her hatred towards people of this skin color is so strong she plans the genocide of White America and seeks to overthrow that country's government and establish her own order."

I hide my surprise behind a solemn facial expression. I never told anyone that; those were only the plans in my mind. Is it possible for the other gods to read my thoughts?

Ra turns to Isis and scowls at her." How do you answer this charge Isis?" he requests.

Isis walks away from me and addresses the elders. I watch her every step and listen to her every word of her defense.

"Elders, the reasons why Isis allowed hatred in her heart were not malicious." Isis replies. "If you review that same chronicle of events, you will see that she was defending herself against a mob of killers who murdered her husband and son. Furthermore, you will see that the culture of this land is one of hatred and division. The White people in this country falsely believe themselves superior to everyone and oppress Negroes. Isis skin was the same color as those who were Negro so she was oppressed like all those in the Negro caste."

"Elders, no matter what justification the Queen makes for the goddess' actions, the fact of the matter is we cannot allow Isis to continue walking among mortals in her current emotional state." Thoth continues. "With such hatred inside her and the power she wields, the goddess could lay waste to mankind and the world."

"I will agree with part of Thoth's argument." Isis replies. "In her current emotional state Isis cannot be allowed to walk among mortals."

The crowd gasps in awe. I stay calm. I know she's going somewhere with this argument; she has to be. Self-incriminating statements from the defense have to have something positive behind them.

"You do know you are incriminating the goddess with such a statement." The stone-faced elder god says.

"Yes I am." Isis replies. "In her current hate filled emotional state Isis is a danger not only to mankind but herself as well. The tragic deaths of her husband and son have left her in a tremendous amount of grief. Isis mistakenly believes the only way to deal with that pain is through a misguided campaign of genocidal mass murder. We must help her deal grieve her losses in a constructive manner."

"Then you are admitting guilt to this charge?" The cloud haired woman asks.

"Yes." Isis replies. "However, before you make your final judgment I ask you to consider the long-standing good record of Isis. For almost two eons she has lived among mortals in peace. Unaware of her Heliopolitan heritage and power she has faithfully served the people of Nubia. Even in America where she suffered unjust treatment, Isis still served her fellow man helping those less fortunate gain the skills needed to achieve a better life. Rather than seek a position of power, she humbly decided to share her centuries of knowledge as a schoolteacher. This is only one dark period in her life. She will have centuries more of brighter ones."

"This goddess is the second coming of Seth." Thoth continues. "In time she could even come after us. Let us execute her before she brings death and suffering to us."

"Isis is definitely not the danger Seth was." Isis says walking over to me. "Seth was a malevolent god who embraced the hatred inside him and sought to use his power to overthrow the kingdom of Old Heliopolis through a treasonous war campaign. Isis is a grieving mother and wife who has made an error in judgment. Isis did not act with malice of forethought the way Seth did. Misguided by her anger she acted impulsively. She never learned the ways of the gods and only applied the violent philosophies she learned as a mortal to her life. Now that Isis is among us we have an opportunity to correct the behavior she has learned and teach her a way that is right."

"Do you believe there is a chance to redeem this goddess Isis?" The gray haired god sitting on the right end of bench asks.

"Yes, I believe there is a tremendous opportunity for her redemption." Isis answers. "It was our irresponsible decision to abandon Isis that led to her adopting these reprobate mortal values. However, she has not gone too far astray despite her upbringing. Isis has done many good deeds. I believe she will continue to serve both mankind and god once she learns the right way."

"She is born of a mortal woman and walked among men." Thoth continues. "The nature of man is savage and reprobate. If we allow one such as this among us she could corrupt us."

"Isis may be flesh on the outside but she is a goddess on the inside." Isis replies. "And the nature of a goddess is loving and just. Isis has a good soul. She will be no threat to any creature once she is redeemed."

Maybe to flies and mosquitoes that bother me in the summer. I think she's persuading them. The two Elders on the left end and the cloud haired woman seem to be entertaining Isis' redemption arguments. They listen attentively to everything she says. Even Osiris cracks a smile briefly before returning to an indifferent expression. However, Ra and the stone-faced man aren't convinced. They continue to scowl at Isis and me. She still has a lot of persuading to do.

Ra and Thoth look at each other funny. I guess neither can argue any more points about this charge. For everything they toss at her Isis has an answer to it.

Elders, I rest my case on this charge." Thoth says.

"Isis do you seek to continue?" Ra asks.

"We rest our case on this charge as well." Isis says.

"Present your evidence on the second count Thoth." Ra requests.

"Elders, Isis has forsaken her Heliopolitan heritage and now worships another God. Instead of practicing our religion she follows the teachings of the Christ and his Father the unknown unnamed God. Furthermore, she believes in the resurrection of this Christ. You only need ask her and she will admit to this."

Ra turns to me. "Do you worship this God?"

I won't give Isis a chance to answer for me this time. I don't care if it kills me I will never deny my Lord. "Yes. I believe in God and I believe that Jesus is his son." I answer.

The gods sitting in the pews gasp in awe. I'll say it again and I'll say it louder for all of them to hear it. They may have legal jurisdiction over me, but they have no spiritual jurisdiction over me. As a citizen of New Heliopolis, I will obey their laws but they will not impose their religion on me.

"Do you also believe in the resurrection of the Christ?" Thoth asks.

"Yes I do." I answer.

"I rest my case on this count Elders." Thoth answers smiling at me. "The goddess has confessed to it."

"How do you answer this charge Isis?" Ra requests.

Isis seems unfazed by my confession. She presses on with her defense. "Elders, Isis was born in a time when we were no longer being worshipped regularly. There were few temples to us and fewer that practiced regularly. So she would not know of our religion."

"The Nubian royalty practiced our religion." Thoth continues.

"Didn't you rest your case?" Queen Isis asks.

"Counsel has the right to rebut the defense's arguments." Thoth replies smugly.

Isis gives him a sly look. "Isis was a slave during this era." She says. "And slaves throughout Egypt and Nubia had no access to the temples like royalty did. Because of the limited access to our temples people of the lower classes throughout both lands practiced many religions, not just Christianity."

"It is not natural for a goddess to serve another God."

"I believe that it is a good thing Isis is a part of the Christian faith." Isis continues. "By practicing the philosophies of peace and goodwill Christ teaches Isis hasn't become completely corrupted by the values of mortals."

"You speak highly of this unknown, unnamed God. Do you believe in him Isis?" Thoth asks

"Yes." Isis says smiling at me.

"Elders, our Queen's statement is heresy!" Thoth exclaims. "A god is only supposed to believe in their own power and that of Great Ra. Our authority is divine and must be respected above all in New Heliopolis." Thoth says.

"Our power is divine in New Heliopolis." Isis answers. "However it is not divine in other parts of the world nor is it truly supreme to all. America is a country where our power is not seen as divine. In this land and many parts of the world, the Unknown God Isis worships is divine and supreme."

"More heresy!" Thoth exclaims. "Perhaps we have the wrong goddess Isis on trial. I suggest we bring this trial to a quick close before our Queen convicts herself of a crime."

"What crimes have I committed in stating facts?" Isis continues. "We have never deemed ourselves as the one true set of supreme gods nor can we claim to be as powerful as the Unknown God. Even during the age of the Pharaohs our power was proven not to be supreme."

"In Egypt we were utterly omnipotent. We even deemed the Pharaoh to be a god himself." Thoth says.

"Would Pharaoh Ramses II army drowned in the Red Sea in his quest to slaughter the Hebrews if our power were completely omnipotent?" Isis replies. "That one event proves the existence of the Unknown God and it proves that he is infinitely more powerful than we are."

For a moment there is nothing but silence in the room. Ra looks angry enough to spit and Thoth looks flabbergasted. She's got them there. There's no way they can prove her wrong with the facts right in front of them.

"We're getting off track here." Thoth says. "It is against our law for one of our own citizens to worship this God. Whether she be a lost child or a Queen of New Heliopolis all must be punished who violate the statute."

"You elders would have a hard time punishing all those who did not follow this law." Isis defends. "Besides Isis and myself, you would have to punish many generations of Egyptians who would be guilty of forsaking us as the supreme power. Even before the Romans conquered Egypt, many Egyptians abandoned the Heliopolitan faith and took up other religions."

"What is your point Isis?" Ra asks. "The law is still on the books."

"The law is still on the books in the ruins of Old Heliopolis and the citizens who violate it New Heliopolis never had any knowledge of it." Isis answers. "Would you punish them for disobeying a law they weren't aware they were violating?"

"No." Ra concedes. "It would be a waste of this court's time."

"It would also be a waste of this court's time now to punish Isis for a violating the law when you have not punished the billions before her who have broken it." Isis says.

Thoth becomes frustrated. "Isis, you speak heresy and you twist our history only to further incriminate the goddess. What is the purpose of this defense?"

Isis smiles at him before answering. "We have never insisted that any citizen of Old Heliopolis, New Heliopolis, or Egypt worship us. Since the beginnings of the times of man, what god people have worshipped has always been their individual choice. During the time of Ramses, the Hebrew slaves practiced their faith freely in our land. Isis has the right to worship the same God now. With that I rest my case on this charge."

Osiris nods his head after hearing Isis speak. She must have gotten something right if he's agreeing with her.

A long silence passes. Ra and the Elder gods quietly confer among themselves briefly before addressing us.

"Have you both presented satisfactory evidence in your arguments on the charges?" Ra asks.

"Yes Elders." Thoth answers.

"Yes Elders." Isis replies.

"Present your closing statement Thoth." Ra requests.

"Elders, by the words of her own counsel and the confession of her own mouth, the goddess Isis is clearly guilty on both counts. With hatred in her heart towards White Americans, she plans the genocide of the White race of American people and would have replaced the government of the country with one to suit her views. She worships another God and refuses to acknowledge our power as supreme; confessing with her own mouth that Jesus is the Christ, God his Father and their power Supreme. I say to you that this goddess is a menace to both man and god, and we have not seen a terror like this one since the days of Seth. She is too much of a danger to keep alive. The only way to make sure she harms no one is with an execution by beheading."

The crowd is quiet after Thoth speaks. It seems they weren't convinced with his arguments.

"Present your closing statement Isis." Ra requests.

"Elders, we concede guilt on both of these counts." Isis begins. "However, the facts presented to you do not warrant such an extreme penalty. You do not want to execute a mother who is grieving over the loss of her husband and firstborn son. Isis' actions were defensive not malicious, if any of us were in her situation we would be vulnerable to the same misguided anger towards these White Americans she feels. I propose a constructive punishment that fits the crimes committed one that corrects the behavior that makes Isis a danger. I ask you to give Isis an opportunity to redeem herself from these terrible deeds she has done. She needs time to work through her grief and anger. Once we help her face this tragedy you will see that Isis is not malevolent like Seth. As a Christian she follows the ways of peace and goodwill, and tries to help others with her centuries of knowledge. She has the potential to do much more for both man and god, but only if you allow her an opportunity to do so through redemption."

"Is that all counsel?" Ra asks.

"That is all." Isis says.

"Court is in recess."

The gods sitting in the pews remain in the courtroom while the Elders leave through the gold doors behind their bench. Thoth and the woman with the feather in her hair follow behind them carrying the transcripts of the trial.

While the elders prepare to deliberate, Osiris smiles at Queen Isis. He's proud of her; so am I. I think she convinced them to see things her way.

Osiris jumps out of his throne and rushes through the doors the elders went through. Where's he's off to in such a hurry?

Chapter 10

I dash through the library headed for the display case. I'm going to share my gifts with Isis before she goes away.

When I reach the case I take a moment to think about what to give her. I want her to have the same hope I have when I come here. However, these are weapons of war and most of them wouldn't be appropriate for me to give her in the courtroom. If the verdict is death, she may prove the elders right and use them against us.

No, I can't think negatively. I know my wife convinced the elders to spare my daughter's life. There has to be something here I can share with Isis right now.

I glance at the gold gauntlets hanging beneath the shield. These will be appropriate; she can't to harm anyone or herself with them. I open the case and pull the smooth gold braclets from the display. I hope they'll inspire her to think of the future.

The gauntlets will give her hope, however Isis needs to grieve and deal with her emotions constructively. Writing helped me deal with my feelings in the past. Perhaps a journal would help Isis deal with her feelings as well.

I gesture my left hand and a book filled with blank pages appears in my palm. Tucked in the front cover is a pen. With my power I enchant the journal to never run out of pages and this pen to never run out of ink. I hurry out of the library and race to the courtroom. I hope the elders have not passed sentence on Isis yet.

Chapter 11

While the elders deliberate my fate, I stand silently and wait for my conviction. I feel at peace with myself about everything. I thank God I'm not going to die today.

Isis beams with joy while the other gods congratulate her on her defense. She should be proud; that was one tremendous case she put together in the matter of a day. In my opinion she won a losing argument.

I wonder where Osiris ran off to. When the Elders left to deliberate, he scurried out of here like his tail was on fire. Perhaps the rat wanted to find a place to hide so he wouldn't have to hear that I'm going to live. I wonder when that mouse will ever act like a man.

The gold doors open; I get tense anticipating the entrance of the Elder gods. I'm surprised when I see Osiris darting through them. What's he doing here? Did he get enough backbone to finish watching my trial or did he think he'd find the perfect hiding spot behind his throne?

Osiris hurries around the bench and into the center of the courtroom. In his hands is a pair of gold bracelets and a book with a pen tucked in the front cover. The awkward grimace he gives me as he approaches makes me scowl back at him.

"Isis." Osiris says. "I want to give you these things."

I want to treat him as cruelly as he's treated me, but the sincere look in his eyes makes me change my attitude towards him. I'll hear what he has to say.

"These bracelets will give you hope." Osiris says handing the smooth gold bands me. "Whenever you look at your reflection them know that one day you will be free."

I slip the bracelets on my wrists. They're so long that they go halfway up my forearms. Once they're on they start to tingle. Maybe it's because the metal is so old. I yank at them to take them off but they won't come off. It's like there's some magic spell on them that keeps them on my wrists.

Osiris smiles as he hands me the hardbound book. I flip through its pages expecting a bible; unfortunately all the pages are blank. There's a pen tucked in a pocket inside the front cover. I give him a thankful smile and he gives me another indifferent look.

"It's always good to keep a journal. It will help you deal with your feelings and put things in perspective." Osiris continues. "When you are redeemed I will come to see you. Perhaps then we can reconcile our relationship."

What- I'm not good enough to be around now! I'm the same person now that I will be later on and you can't love me for that? I guess I'll always be nothing to you.

I hide my disappointment behind a polite smile. I won't let him know how much what he said hurt me. I'll be kind to him instead. Perhaps that will heap some hot coals on his head.

"Thank you." I say quietly.

Osiris shuffles away from me and eases into his throne. Queen Isis walks over to me to find out what we've been talking about.

"Isis, did your father-"

"He just wanted to give me these." I say holding my arms up to show her the bracelets. "And this journal to write in." I say pointing to the book in my hands.

"He's just trying to help."

"I know."

"I want you to know that no matter what happens I'll always love you and I'll always be there for you." Isis says.

I believe her when she says that. The look in her eyes tells me she loves me with all her heart. Spontaneously she gives me a hug. I'm about to hug her back when I see the Elder gods taking their seats behind the bench. The woman with the feather in her hair takes her seat at the table and begins to write on her scroll. Thoth calls the court to order as I break the embrace I share with Isis.

"Court is to come to order." Thoth says. "The Elders have come to a verdict and are ready to pass judgment on the goddess."

I'm calm and relaxed as Ra begins to speak. I look up at him listening attentively to his words regarding my final fate.

"Goddess Isis, come forward." Ra requests.

I walk into the center of the courtroom. My heart races in my chest but I keep my head held high and stare directly into his intense eyes.

"Goddess Isis on the first charge of allowing hatred in your heart we find you guilty." Ra says.

The crowd gasps in shock. I don't react to his words.

"On the second charge of forsaking your heritage and worshipping another god we find you not guilty." Ra replies.

I hear whispers from the spectators regarding the judgment. I remain silent.

"What is the sentence Great Ra?" Thoth asks.

"We cannot allow the goddess in her current emotional state to walk among mortals." Ra says. With hatred in her heart, she is a danger to both man and god. However, her crimes are not as egregious as those of Seth. For that reason alone we shall spare the goddess' life."

I let out a sigh of relief. I'm not going to die.

"Taking into account the numerous good deeds the goddess has done in her *short* lifetime, we will grant the goddess an opportunity to redeem herself." Ra continues. "Until the day when she finds redemption the goddess will be banished to the Island of Solitude where she will not threaten any man, god, or beast. She shall have her power taken from her until the day of that redemption. And from this day forward, the goddess shall never bear another child. Finally, she shall wear the mark of Isis on her to remind her of this trial until the day of her redemption. When the hatred is purged from her soul, then the goddess will be allowed to involve herself with us and the world."

The gods in the pews continue to whisper among themselves about the judgment. Before I can react to his ruling, Ra gets up and points his index finger at me. I scream in terror as the white flame shoots from his hand and scorches my right arm. The pain from the burn is so agonizing I feel it searing through my entire body. As I grab my throbbing arm, I fall to my knees and drop the journal on the floor.

Ra gestures his hand and my body lifts into the air convulsing wildly in a violent twitching spasm. White lightning shoots out of my body and back into Ra's hand. When I collapse onto the floor I feel so weak.

I feel myself blacking out. With my last rush of strength I reach for the journal; when I grab it I everything goes black.

Chapter 12

While the gallery of gods are distracted reacting to the harshness of Ra's punishment I shall use it as an opportunity to take my leave.

I slip through the gold doors in the back of the room and silently close them behind me. I chant quietly to myself and dark magic envelops my body removing the disguise I wore. I feel so much more comfortable in my regular clothes and in my true form. That servant's outfit was a little too short and too tight for my tastes.

With a thought I make a pair of leathery bat wings sprout from my back. A flash of light envelops me as I lean forward and fall into the darkness of the pits of Hell. Once I share this information with my master Lord Seth, he's sure to go along with the scheme I'm planning.

Epilogue

A warm wind stirs me out of my state of unconsciousness. I feel grains of sand on under me and see palm trees a few yards away. This must be the Island of Solitude.

I'm still groggy but I manage to pull myself up. My right arm still throbs from the burn Ra made on it. The skin marked with the symbol is tight, blackened and sore. I think I can work through the enough of the pain though to swim out of here.

"YOU CALL THIS A PRISON!" I mock looking up at the sky. "YOU KNOW I CAN LEAVE ANY TIME I WANT TO!"

Some prison this is, there isn't anything to keep me here. I could return to the world anytime I wished. Ra has no jurisdiction over me; God is my Lord. I think I can find land in a couple of hours of swimming. I race for the shore as fast as I can. Leaping towards the clear ocean water, I crash into the sand before I reach the shore's edge. I don't see anything at all; what's keeping me from leaving?

Air can't be strong as iron bars. I should be able to escape here easily.

"I'M GOING TO FIND A WAY OUT OF HERE! YOU HAVE NO POWER OVER ME! I'M A CHRISTIAN! I DON'T BELIEVE IN YOUR POWER!"

I throw my good shoulder into the invisible wall and the impact of hitting it sends me crashing to the ground. Hard. I better not try that again. I'm already at a temporary handicap with a burned arm. I don't need to incapacitate myself any further by breaking the other.

In my frustration I pick up my journal and toss it at the ocean. I'm surprised when it bounces off the invisible wall and hits me in the back of the head. Lucky for me the only thing bruised is my ego. I'm not going anywhere anytime soon. I may as well get used to this ocean view.

I pick my journal up off the beach and storm over to a nearby palm tree. Sitting under the shade I put all the angry thoughts in my head I'm feeling on paper.

Also Available by Shawn James

The Temptation of John Haynes
ISBN 978-0-615-42592-4
Suggested Retail Price $15.00

Death kills the Flesh.
Compromise Kills the Soul.

All About Marilyn: A Screenplay
ISBN: 978-0615342580
Suggested Retail Price $14.00

Fame Ends at 34.
Life begins at 35.
A story of Hollywood in Black and White.

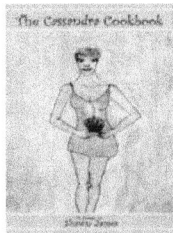

The Cassandra Cookbook
ISBN: 978-1602642294
Suggested Retail Price $14.95

A pinch of hard work.
A dash of determination.
A recipe for success.

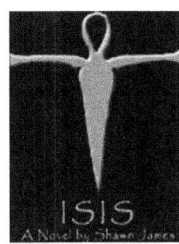

ISIS

ISBN 1-58939-236-1
Suggested Retail Price $12.95

A lost goddess.
A heritage found.
A greater destiny to be achieved.

www.ingramcontent.com/pod-product-compliance
Lightning Source LLC
Chambersburg PA
CBHW071343130626

46556CB00005B/2011